THIS CANDLEWICK BOOK BELONGS TO:

_____

_____

_____

To Bea

First U.S. paperback edition 2013

The Library of Congress has cataloged the hardcover edition as follows:

Lawrence, John, date.
  This little chick / John Lawrence. — 1st U.S. ed.
  p.   cm.
  Summary: A little chick shows that he can make the sounds of the animals in his neighborhood.
  ISBN 978-0-7636-1716-5 (hardcover)
  [1. Chickens — Fiction. 2. Animals — Infancy — Fiction. 3. Animal sounds — Fiction.
  4. Domestic animals — Fiction. 5. Stories in rhyme.] I. Title.
    PZ8.3.L369 Th 2002
    [E] — dc21   2001035633

ISBN 978-0-7636-6350-6 (paperback)

TLF 17 16
10 9 8 7 6

Printed in Dongguan, Guangdong, China

The illustrations in this book were made from
vinyl engravings, watercolor
washes, and printed wood textures.
The words were made from an original
alphabet engraved in vinyl.
Computer technology was used to bring
these hand-crafted elements together.

Candlewick Press
99 Dover Street
Somerville, Massachusetts 02144

visit us at www.candlewick.com

This

John Lawrence

Little Chick

CANDLEWICK PRESS

This little chick from over the way went to play with the pigs one day.

And what do you think
they heard him say?

This little chick from over the way
went to swim with the ducks one day.

And what do you think
they heard him say?

This little chick from over the way
went to laze with the cows one day.

And what do you think
they heard him say?

This little chick from over the way
went to jump with the frogs one day.

And what do you think
they heard him say?

Ribbit
Ribbit
Ribbit
Ribbit
Ribbit

This little chick from over the way
went to skip with the lambs one day.

And what do you think
they heard him say?

Baa

Baa

Baa

Baa

Baa

Baa

This little chick from over the way went home to his mom at the end of the day.

And what do you think
she heard him say?

John Lawrence's intricate wood engravings grace the pages of many classic novels and anthologies. But for *This Little Chick*, he chose to work in vinyl to make large, bold engravings. He says, "I always wanted to do a book for very young children, and I was delighted when a little chick turned up on my doorstep." John Lawrence's other books for children include *Tiny's Big Adventure* and *Sea Horse: The Shyest Fish in the Sea.*